This book belongs to:

_____

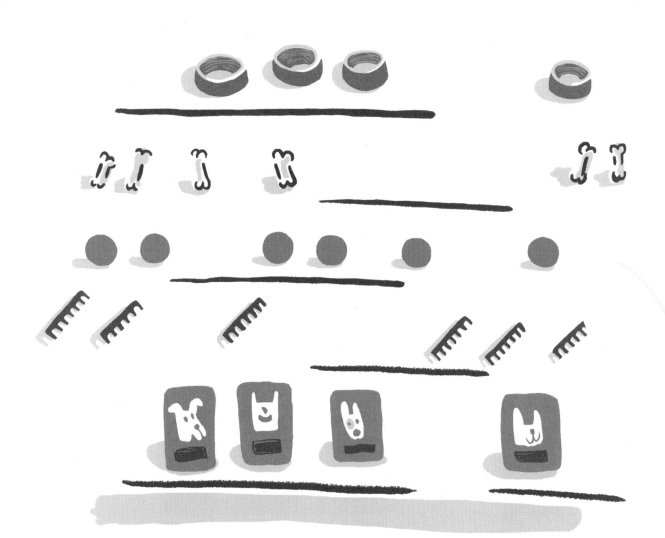

Hey, Boy

Benjamin Strouse

Illustrated by Jennifer Phelan

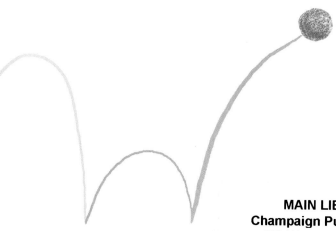

Margaret K. McElderry Books

New York London Toronto Sydney New Delhi

MARGARET K. McELDERRY BOOKS • An imprint of Simon & Schuster Children's Publishing Division • 1230 Avenue of the Americas, New York, New York 10020 • Copyright © 2014, 2017 by Benjamin Strouse • A different version of this book was previously self-published. • All rights reserved, including the right of reproduction in whole or in part in any form. • MARGARET K. McELDERRY BOOKS is a trademark of Simon & Schuster, Inc. • For information about special discounts for bulk purchases, please contact Simon & Schuster Special Sales at 1-866-506-1949 or business@ simonandschuster.com. • The Simon & Schuster Speakers Bureau can bring authors to your live event. For more information or to book an event, contact the Simon & Schuster Speakers Bureau at 1-866-248-3049 or visit our website at www.simonspeakers.com. • Book design by Lauren Rille • The text for this book was set in Prater. • The illustrations for this book were rendered in pen & ink and colored digitally.
Manufactured in China
0217 SCP
First Edition
10 9 8 7 6 5 4 3 2 1
Library of Congress Cataloging-in-Publication Data
Names: Strouse, Benjamin, author. | Phelan, Jennifer, illustrator.
Title: Hey, Boy / Benjamin Strouse ; Illustrated by Jennifer Phelan.
Description: First edition. | New York : Margaret K. McElderry Books, [2017] | Summary: "A little boy must give up his new dog after he gets hurt caring for him, but never gives up on dreams of them being together"—Provided by publisher.
Identifiers: LCCN 2016022296 (print) | LCCN 2016042671 (eBook) | ISBN 9781481471015 (hardcover) | ISBN 9781481471022 (eBook)
Subjects: | CYAC: Dogs—Fiction. | Human-animal relationships—Fiction.
Classification: LCC PZ7.1.S797 He 2017 (print) | LCC PZ7.1.S797 (eBook) | DDC [E]—dc23
LC record available at https://lccn.loc.gov/2016022296

To lovely Ronni,
with whom so much is possible.
—B. S.

To my husband, Gleb,
whom I met and married while making this book
—J. P.

One morning, a boy met a dog.

"Hey, Boy. Do you want to see my house?"

That night, the boy told the dog
about the adventures they would have
and the games they would play.

They couldn't wait to get started.

They played and played like crazy . . .

until the boy got hurt.

"You're not ready to take care
of a dog," his mom said.
"Maybe when you're grown up."

"Don't worry, Boy. I have a plan.

I'm going to grow up faster than anybody!"
said the boy.
"You won't be at the shelter long."

"Stay, Boy."

For more than a month,
the boy tried to grow up
as fast as he could.
But in the meantime . . .

the boy missed the dog so much,

he decided it was okay to visit.

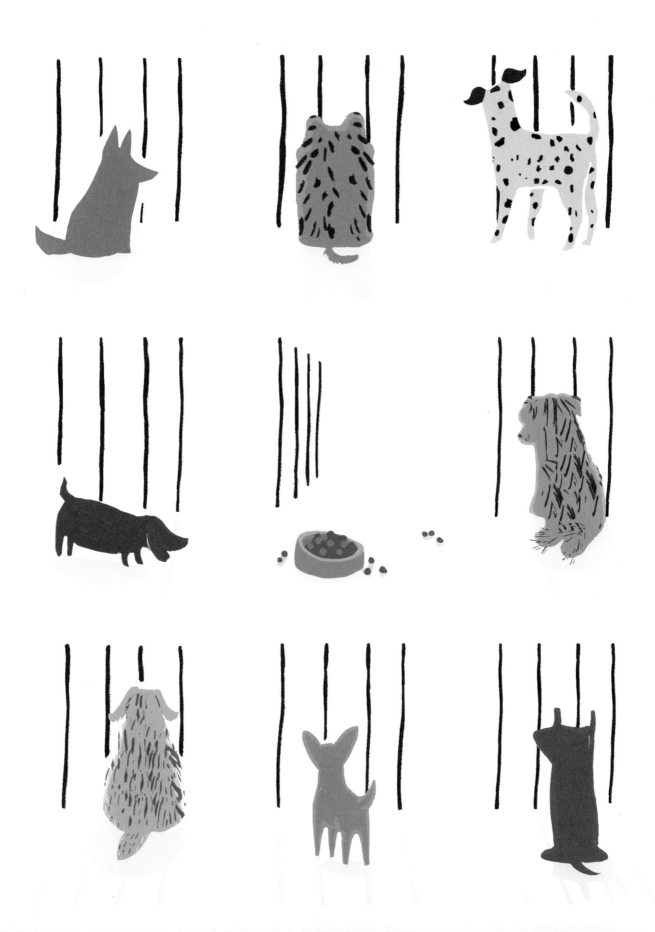

But his friend was gone.

Adopted.

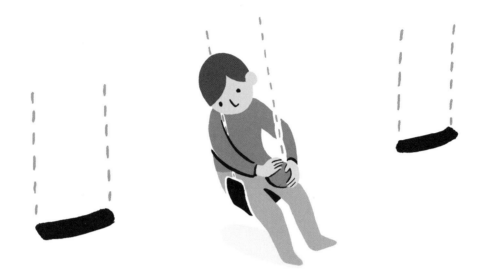

For a while the boy didn't know what to think.

He felt sad.

Until an old-fashioned letter arrived in the mail.
His friend was on an adventure, living somewhere
the boy had never been.

And he was welcome to visit!

"Hey, Boy! You're getting so big!"
They played and played like they had
when they first met, until they were
both exhausted and needed to rest.

"When I finish growing up,"
the boy told the dog,

"we'll live on a farm."

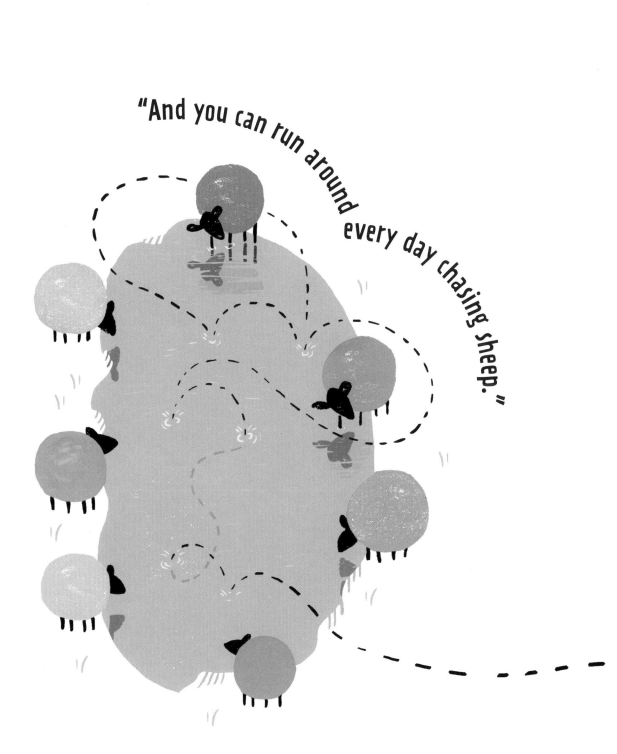

"And you can run around every day chasing sheep."

"I made my own lunch today, so it won't be much longer."

Time passed.

The boy tried harder than ever to grow up.

He wanted to tell his friend everything.

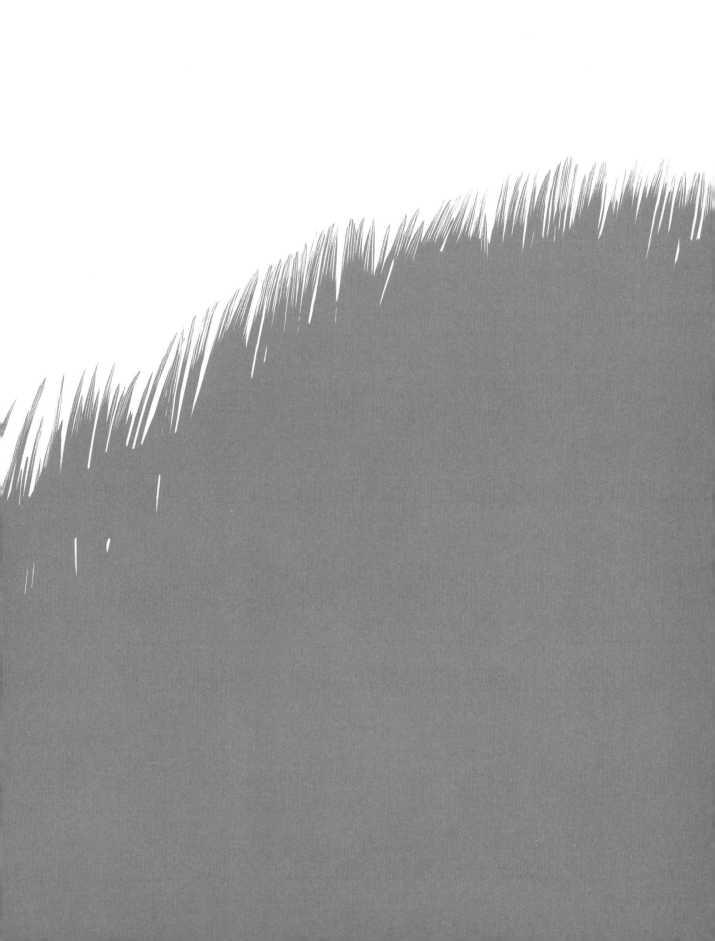

The boy visited whenever he could.

"I biked here," he told the dog.

"I also researched dog food, and the best kind can be eaten by both of us."

"But I haven't tried it. . . ."

Sometimes a while passed between visits.

The dog was older now.
They didn't run around and play
as much as they used to.
"Don't worry, Boy," the boy whispered
at the end of one visit.
"I still love you."

More time passed.

Some days were bad.

Other days were good.

Sometimes nothing seemed to make sense.

Sometimes it did.

But he never stopped missing his friend.

The boy had done it —

grown up.

But he visited less and less.

Then one day there was news.

The couple was no longer young enough

to take care of the dog.

At first the boy didn't know what to think.

He sat down.

Where would his friend live?

But he knew the answer,

and it made him happy.

Ready or not, he was going to bring the dog home.

The boy drove and drove. . . .

When he arrived, he felt nervous.
Even afraid.

What if he doesn't recognize me?

Will he wag his tail?

What if he barks?

"Hey, Boy!"

His friend moved very slowly now.

He couldn't see very well.

But, of course, the dog was happy.

And the boy was overjoyed.

"Thank you," he said.

So the boy told his friend about the
adventures they would have.

And the games they would play

and play

and play.